First published 1985 by
Deans International Publishing
Copyright © 1985 Victoria House Publishing Ltd.
This edition published 1989 by
Colour Library Books Ltd,
Godalming, Surrey, England.
ISBN 0 86283 663 8

Printed in the German Democratic Republic

LITTLE MOUSE'S
BEDTIME
STORIES

Written by Lis Taylor
Illustrated by Colin Petty

Colour Library Books

Contents

The Dancing Class

"Time for your dancing class," called Mrs Mouse up the stairs. Little Mouse came slowly down with her ballet shoes hanging over one arm.

"I don't know what's the matter with you," said Mrs Mouse as she put on her coat. "You used to look forward to your class."

It was true. Little Mouse had loved dancing at first. But then Miss Tiptoes had told them they had to practise hard for the show they were to put on for their parents and Little Mouse found it very hard to remember all her steps.

"Don't worry," said her mummy, giving her a big hug as she left her at the door of the dancing school. "Just follow what everyone else does if you can't remember."

Little Mouse tried copying Skippy Bunny who was in front of her and she found that was much better. She could keep up with the class.

"Very good, Little Mouse," said Miss Tiptoes. "You must have been practising at home. Now I want everyone to dance by themselves this time. One at a time, please."

They all stood in line and Little Mouse watched very carefully, trying hard to remember what the others did, but when it came to her turn she found everything had just gone out of her head.

"Come on, Little Mouse," said Miss Tiptoes, looking up from the piano. "I'll start playing again. One two three ..."

As Miss Tiptoes played, Little Mouse started to dance. She couldn't remember the steps, so she just made it up as she went along. Miss Tiptoes kept on playing, but her eyes opened wider and wider.

"Where did you learn that dance?" she asked when Little Mouse had finished.

"I made it up," said Little Mouse, feeling a bit scared. She was sure Miss Tiptoes was going to be cross.

"It was very good!" said Miss Tiptoes. "Very good indeed. I want you to do that dance in the show instead of dancing with everybody else. You will do your own solo!"

Little Mouse was very pleased, and Mrs Mouse was surprised to find that she seemed very keen to go dancing again. And do you know, Little Mouse never ever forgot a single step. Her solo dance went perfectly and all the parents clapped and clapped.

Auntie Flo's Birthday

They were all making baskets at school. Timmy Mouse didn't like doing it.

"I don't see the point," he said. "I won't *use* it afterwards."

"You could give it to someone as a present," suggested Little Squirrel, but Timmy didn't think anyone would want it. He finished making it all the same and took it home after school.

"Oh, there you are, Timmy," said Mrs Mouse. "You haven't forgotten that your Auntie Flo is coming to tea, have you? Pop up and change."

"Hello, my dears!" said Auntie Flo when she arrived, hugging Timmy so hard that his ears went red!

"Come and have some tea," said Mrs Mouse, leading the way into the living room.

"Gosh!" thought Timmy. "Mummy's really spoiling Auntie Flo." There was a huge plate of sandwiches, crisps, nuts and a large fruit salad.

"That was splendid," said Auntie Flo, when she had eaten as much as she could.

"Oh, you can't finish just yet," said Mrs Mouse. "We've got a surprise!" She opened the larder and brought out a beautiful birthday cake covered in candles.

"Oh no! I'd forgotten all about Auntie Flo's birthday," thought Timmy. "Everyone else will have a present and I haven't anything to give!"

While Auntie Flo blew out the candles Timmy raced upstairs. He'd just had a brilliant idea! He ran back into the kitchen with a hurriedly wrapped parcel.

"Happy birthday, Auntie Flo," he said, breathlessly.

Auntie Flo unwrapped the basket that Timmy had made at school that day. He was sure she wouldn't like it—but Auntie was delighted!

"It will make a perfect fruit basket," she said. "I will keep it on the little table by the fire and whenever you come to see me you can just help yourself!"

11

Shopping on Wheels

Little Mouse was very pleased with her new roller skates. Every day she took them down to the playground and practised so she was getting very good.

One day, as she was on her way to the playground with her skates hung over her shoulder, she met Grandma Squirrel who was struggling up the hill from Mrs Badger's shop with a very heavy bag of shopping.

"I don't think I should have bought so much," Grandma told her. "This bag is almost too heavy to carry. I think I'll pop into Mrs Bunny's for a cup of tea and a chat. Maybe I'll be strong enough to carry it home after that."

Little Mouse felt sorry for Grandma Squirrel. "You call in for a cup of tea," she said, "and I'll take your shopping home."

"But you're far too small to carry it," argued Grandma.

"Don't worry," said Little Mouse. "I've got a very good idea. The shopping won't seem heavy at all."

Grandma was puzzled, but off she went for her cup of tea.

When she arrived home later she was surprised to see her big shopping bag sitting in the kitchen, but no sign of Grandpa Squirrel or Little Mouse. Then she heard some banging from the garden shed.

"Whatever is all that noise?" thought Grandma Squirrel. But when she went to find out, Grandpa Squirrel wouldn't let her into the shed.

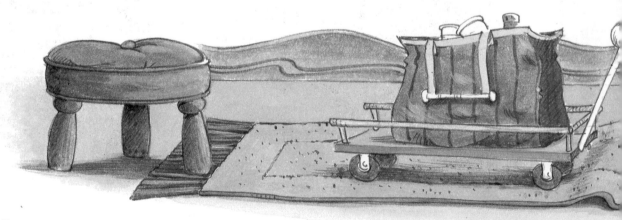

12

"I'll be ready in five minutes and then you can see what I've been making," he said.

At last Grandpa came out, pushing a small wooden trolley on four little wheels.

"What is it?" asked Grandma.

Grandpa said nothing, but picked up Grandma's shopping bag and put it on the trolley.

"There! Try pushing that," he told her.

Grandma pushed it up and down with cries of delight. "Why, it's so easy to push! I'll have no trouble getting the shopping home now! However did you think of such a thing?"

"I didn't," said Grandpa. "It was Little Mouse who gave me the idea when she brought your shopping home tied on top of her roller skates!"

"So that's how she did it!" said Grandma. "Clever Little Mouse!"

At the Swimming Pool

Mrs Mouse was taking Little Mouse, Timmy and Little Squirrel to the swimming pool. It was a lovely hot day and Mrs Mouse was wearing her new, flowery sun hat.

Just then there was a little gust of wind and the hat flew off Mrs Mouse's head and landed over the hedge. Everyone laughed and Timmy ran to fetch it.

"You'd better be careful or you'll lose it," he told Mrs Mouse.

But Mrs Mouse's hat just wouldn't stay on. It blew off twice before they reached the pool.

"I expect it will be all right now," she said, settling down beside the pool. "It's nice and sheltered here."

Little Mouse, Little Squirrel and Timmy all got changed and Little Mouse dived into the water.

"Come on," she called to Little Squirrel. But Little Squirrel stayed on the side of the pool.

"Whatever's the matter?" asked Little Mouse.

Little Squirrel explained that she had never learnt to swim.

"It's shallow enough to paddle," said Little Mouse. "So it doesn't matter if you can't swim."

But Little Squirrel thought she would just watch for a bit and

she sat on the side while Little Mouse and Timmy swam up and down the pool. Each time they passed, Little Mouse called to her to come in but Little Squirrel shook her head. Somehow she felt afraid of the water.

"Never mind, dear, you just sit here and have a chat with me," said Mrs Mouse kindly.

But as she spoke there was a sudden gust of wind and Mrs Mouse gave a little cry as her hat blew off yet again. This time it flew straight towards the swimming pool.

"I'll get it!" cried Little Squirrel, jumping up. She leapt high in the air and just managed to catch the hat. She came down again with a big splash and was surprised to see that she had jumped right into the pool.

"Well done!" cried Mrs Mouse, taking hold of her hat.

"Brave Little Squirrel!" said Little Mouse. "Fancy jumping in the water."

"You know, it's really rather nice," said Little Squirrel, spashing about a bit. "I think perhaps I'd like to learn to swim after all!"

The Painting Trip

One summer afternoon Mr Mole took the class on a painting trip. They all set off with their paints and brushes and paper to find a nice sunny spot where they could do nature paintings.

"You can paint whatever you like," Mr Mole told them. "It could be a tree, some flowers—anything at all."

Little Mouse had seen a butterfly basking in the sun and she thought it would make a lovely picture. She took out her paints very quietly so she wouldn't disturb it.

She was doing very well for a few minutes, but then the butterfly decided to fly off. Little Mouse picked up her things and chased after it.

It landed on a big, purple thistle and poor Little Mouse got very prickled as she climbed through the thistle patch to reach her butterfly.

She managed to colour in one wing and then it flew off again, this time up to the branch of a tree.

"Oh dear," said Little Mouse to herself as she climbed up. "It isn't very easy painting up a tree."

But she didn't stay there long. The butterfly was soon off again, this time so fast that Little Mouse had to run so she didn't lose sight of it.

She was running so fast that she didn't have time to look where she was going and suddenly she felt her feet sinking into the ground. A moment later she had fallen flat on her face in the middle of a boggy bit of ground.

Once she had wiped the mud from her eyes she looked round for the butterfly. It was nowhere to be seen. Poor Little Mouse! She took her half-finished painting and went back to join the others.

Mr Mole couldn't help laughing when he saw her covered in the mud. "You look like a nature painting yourself!" he told her. "And I think you deserve a special prize for choosing such a hard picture to paint."

Back at school, Mr Mole went to his cupboard and took out a beautiful picture of a butterfly just like the one that Little Mouse had been painting.

Little Mouse was very pleased. She was able to finish her picture and then she hung them both side by side in her bedroom.

Chasing Rainbows

Little Bunny, Little Mouse, Little Squirrel and Little Owl had all agreed to meet at the big tree in the wood. As Little Squirrel made her way there, she saw a beautiful big rainbow arching across the sky.

"I wonder where the end of the rainbow is?" she said to the others when they were gathered round the foot of the tree.

"There's supposed to be all kinds of good things at the end of the rainbow," said Little Owl.

"Why don't we try to find it, then?" suggested Little Bunny.

The rainbow seemed to disappear behind some bushes beside Mr Toad's house. They set off through the wood, looking up at the rainbow all the time to make sure they didn't lose sight of it.

After what seemed to be a long time, the four friends arrived at the bushes beside Mr Toad's house and started to look for the end of the rainbow. It was nowhere to be seen.

"It must have moved!" moaned Little Owl.

"Look, there it is," shouted Little Squirrel, pointing to the next hill, towards her grandpa's house. And, sure enough, the tail of the rainbow disappeared behind the hill, in between two tall trees.

The path to Grandpa Squirrel's house was a very wiggly one,

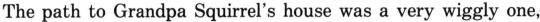

and it was hard to see the rainbow all the time. The sun was shining but it was raining, too. Soon Little Bunny's ears were quite wet and Little Mouse's whiskers were sticking to her face.

At last they reached Grandpa Squirrel's house and looked up for the rainbow. "Oh no!" they all shouted together, for the rainbow had moved again, and now seemed to be vanishing behind Hollyholt Stores.

They sat down outside Grandpa Squirrel's house to think what to do. Then Grandpa came out and they told him all about the rainbow chase.

"Oh, dear me!" laughed Grandpa. "The end of the rainbow indeed! You'll be hunting for ever. But I'm glad you're here because I spent yesterday picking plums from my tree and there are plenty for you to share."

So they spent the rest of the afternoon eating Grandpa's plums, washed down with some home-made lemonade.

"It looks like we found the end of the rainbow after all!" laughed Little Squirrel.

Mrs Prickles Sees a Ghost

Little Owl, Nippy Shrew and Tom Prickles were playing tag after school. At last they all felt tired and sat down on the grass.

"I'm starving," said Nippy.

"Let's get something to eat then," said Tom. "We'll creep into my mummy's bakery and see if there are any buns."

So they crept quietly through the kitchen door. They could hear Mrs Prickles talking to a customer in the shop.

"Yes, I've got some sunflower buns," she said. "I'll just fetch them from the kitchen."

"Quick! Hide!" said Tom, crawling under the table. Little Owl followed him, but there wasn't room for Nippy. He lifted the lid of a big bin and jumped inside.

Mrs Prickles went back into the shop. Tom and Little Owl came out from under the table and looked all around for Nippy.

"Where are you, Nippy?" called Tom in a whisper.

Tom jumped in surprise when he saw the lid of the flour bin move. It slid back and a ghostly white figure appeared. It was Nippy, covered from head to toe in flour.

"Aaagh!" screamed Little Owl and he and Tom ran off as fast as they could—just as Mrs Prickles came rushing in to see what all the noise was about.

She saw the white figure and she screamed too, then went running into the shop shouting, "Ghost! I've seen a ghost!"

Nippy hopped down from the flour bin and shook all the flour off. He helped himself to six sunflower buns (two for each of them) and ran off as fast as he could to find the others. When he explained what had happened they laughed and laughed.

Mrs Prickles never found out what really happened, which is probably just as well because she still enjoys telling customers about the ghost that ate six of her sunflower buns!

Little Bunny's Coconut

There was a fair on the village green. There were roundabouts with brightly painted horses, stalls selling candyfloss and toffee apples, and lots of games where you could win prizes.

Little Bunny wanted to win a coconut. Every year he tried, but he never managed it. This year, he told himself, he really would win one.

First he tried the coconut shy, where you had to hit a coconut

onto the ground by throwing balls at it. The coconut didn't even wobble.

"I think they're stuck on," said Little Bunny, but Little Mouse knocked one off.

On another stall there were lots of prizes—lollipops, teddies, jars of jam *and* coconuts. All you had to do was throw a hoop over something and you won it. Easy!

Little Bunny's first hoop hit the top of a jam jar and fell to the ground. His second hoop went right over the stall and hit Nippy Shrew who was standing behind it.

"Only one hoop left," thought Little Bunny. "I must be very careful." He aimed at a coconut right in the middle and. . . .

"Yes!" cried the stall owner. "You've won a prize."

Little Bunny was very excited. But his ring hadn't gone over the coconut after all. The stall owner handed him a toffee apple instead.

"Well, at least I've won something," said Little Bunny to himself, as he walked slowly towards the exit sign.

Just then he bumped into Little Mouse, who was looking very sad.

"What's the matter, Little Mouse?" asked Little Bunny.

"Oh, nothing, really," said Little Mouse. "It's just that I wanted a toffee apple and I've saved my money until now, but there are none left!"

"Never mind," said Little Bunny. "You can have this one," and he gave her the toffee apple he'd won.

"You *are* kind," said Little Mouse, "but you must have my prize in return," and she handed him a big, brown coconut.

As they walked home together, Little Mouse and Little Bunny agreed it had been the best fair ever.

The End-of-Term Treat

It was the end of the school term and Mr Mole had promised everyone a special end-of-term treat.

"I wonder if it's a picnic?" said Little Bunny, excitedly.

"But why did Mr Mole ask us to bring a reel of cotton and a sewing needle to school today?" asked Little Squirrel.

"Mr Mole has asked Mr Coggles to invent something and we're all to help," said Nippy Shrew, who always seemed to be the first to know anything.

Suddenly there was a loud knock at the door. It was Mr Coggles. He was carrying a big sack and his inventor's notebook.

"Good morning, class," he said. "In this sack there are lots of pieces of material, all in different colours. I want you each to choose your favourite colour and then we can start."

Little Squirrel chose a red piece. Little Bunny chose blue, and all the others chose a colour until the sack was empty.

"Now," said Mr Coggles, looking in his notebook, "you have to sew the colours together. Yellow must be sewn to blue. Blue must be sewn to green and green must be sewn to red . . ." and on he went. At last all the colours were sewn together and the invention lay in a heap on the classroom floor.

"Whatever is it?" asked Little Bunny.

"It looks like a huge bedspread," said Little Mouse.

Mr Coggles spoke. "Tomorrow I want you all to bring your parents to the village green and then you will see what we've invented."

The next morning there was a big crowd on the village green.

"Oh, it's lovely! Look! Look!" shouted Little Bunny, pointing.

24

All the villagers were amazed. There on the green was a huge hot-air balloon, swaying in the breeze. It had a basket fitted below it, and Mr Coggles was sitting inside, waving to them.

"That's right," said Mr Coggles. "You all helped to make this balloon and now you can each have a turn to fly in it over the tree-tops. Isn't this an exciting end-of-term treat!"

Everyone cheered Mr Coggles for being so clever. "Hooray!" they shouted. "Three cheers for the holiday hot-air balloon!"

Little Mouse Goes Haymaking

In the summer holidays Little Mouse went to stay with her cousin Zilly and her Aunt and Uncle Twitcher. They were harvest mice who lived right on the edge of a big hay field.

"You've come at just the right time," Uncle Twitcher told her. "Tomorrow we start haymaking and we need all the help we can get."

The next morning all the Twitchers' friends and relations were out in the field, some cutting the hay, others bundling it up to put onto the hay cart. Little Mouse was on top of the cart with Zilly,

catching the bundles as they were thrown and piling them up. It was hard work in the hot sun and Little Mouse was very glad when Aunt Twitcher appeared with milk and sandwiches.

"Are you feeling tired?" asked Zilly, as they climbed down from the cart.

26

"I certainly am!" replied Little Mouse, who looked rather red.

"Well don't worry. We'll have a rest after lunch and the sun will be cooler by then too," said Zilly kindly.

They ate their lunch, then everyone crept off to find a nice, shady place to rest. Uncle Twitcher blew his whistle when it was time to get back to work.

"Where's Little Mouse?" asked Aunt Twitcher.

"I don't know," said Zilly. "I'm sure she'll be back soon."

But Little Mouse didn't come back at all that afternoon and by tea time Aunt Twitcher was beginning to worry about her.

"We'll take the cart back and unload it," said Uncle Twitcher. "And if she still isn't back we'll go out searching for her."

Uncle Twitcher unloaded the hay and threw the bundles up to Aunt Twitcher and Zilly in the hayloft. He was getting near the end when he stopped and called, "Look at this!"

Aunt Twitcher and Zilly leaned forward to look down into the hay cart. There, curled up in a gap between two bundles of hay, was Little Mouse, fast asleep!

Daisy Chains

Little Squirrel and Little Mouse were making daisy chains. Little Mouse wasn't enjoying it much.

"What's the point of making daisy chains," she moaned. "You can't *do* anything with them."

"It's just fun," said Little Squirrel. "Did you know that daisies are really called 'day's eyes' because they open in the day and close up tight at night?"

She was about to say something more when a tiny wren landed with a plop right on her daisy chain. It flapped and squeaked, "Peep, peep, peep!"

"It's just a baby," said Little Squirrel. "Do you think it has

28

fallen out of its nest?''

"I expect so," said Little Mouse. "But we can't fly so we can't take it back there. We'll just have to look after it until its mummy or daddy comes back."

Little Squirrel made a hammock out of her daisy chain. She twisted the stalks in and out until she had made a fine bed for the little bird. Then they rocked the baby wren to sleep. Very soon Mrs Wren returned. She was very upset when she found one of her babies missing.

"It's all right, Mrs Wren," called Little Mouse. "Your baby is safe down here."

Mrs Wren flew down and was very pleased to see her baby, but then she looked worried.

"How can I get her back to the nest?" she asked.

They all thought for a few minutes and then Little Squirrel said, "I've got a plan! Give me your daisy chain, Little Mouse."

She tied Little Mouse's daisy chain to the hammock and told Mrs Wren to fly up to the nest holding the end in her beak.

The baby wren was back at home before it woke up!

"There!" said Little Squirrel to Little Mouse, "daisy chains can be useful after all!"

Mr Owl's Tidy Garden

Mr Owl had been working hard in his garden. The grass was cut short, the flower-beds were neat and there was not a single weed in sight. Even the flowers grew in straight rows.

Now it was autumn and the leaves started to fall. Mr Owl's tidy lawn was littered with leaves. Every morning he went out with his broom and swept them up. But as soon as he turned his back the leaves started to fall again. It was an endless job and Mr Owl felt very tired of it.

One day as he was busy sweeping, Mr Squirrel popped round with a few chrysanthemums that he had grown.

"I don't know how you find the time to keep everywhere so tidy," said Mr Squirrel. "It's funny though, I feel there's something missing from your garden. I can't say what it is—just something missing."

That afternoon, as Mr Owl was planting his chrysanthemums, Mr Squirrel came running into his garden carrying a sack.

"I've realised what's missing!" he said. "Your garden is *too* tidy." And he ran round and round shaking out leaves from his sack, until the grass and the brown flower-beds were a patchwork of gold and bronze and rusty red.

Mr Owl stood there with his mouth wide open, not knowing what to say. Then Mrs Owl opened the window and called, "It's beautiful, Mr Squirrel. I knew there was something missing!"

Mr Owl scratched his head. "I suppose it does look rather nice actually." And he started to laugh.

After that Mr Owl stopped sweeping up the leaves, and his garden was more beautiful than ever.

Trick and Treat

It was Halloween and Mr Mole had been reading the class some ghost stories.

"Now it's your turn," he said. "I want you to write a story about Halloween."

After lunch they all read out their stories. It was a lot of fun hearing about the witches and monsters that they had made up.

"Do you think there really are ghosts and witches?" Little Squirrel asked Little Mouse.

"No! They're only in stories," said Little Mouse.

All the same, she couldn't help wishing it wasn't quite so dark as she walked home from school that day.

"Thank goodness I'm nearly home," she told herself. But suddenly she saw a strange orange head coming towards her. It was glowing in the dark and smiling. Little Mouse screamed and ran as fast as she could until she was safely inside her own house.

"I saw a . . . a . . . monster," she told her mummy.

Mrs Mouse didn't seem worried. "It's Halloween," she said. "Everybody thinks they see things on Halloween."

Just then there was a knock at the door and Little Mouse went to answer it. She opened the door, gave a big scream, and shut it again quickly.

"Whatever's the matter?" asked Mrs Mouse.

"It's the monster!" cried Little Mouse. "It just knocked at the door."

Mrs Mouse smiled. "I think we should let it in, then. It might want some tea," she said.

"No, no," cried Little Mouse, hiding behind her mummy.

The monster was a big, hollowed out pumpkin. It had cut-out eyes and a mouth and a nightlight inside to make it glow.

"Hello!" said Timmy, who was holding the pumpkin. "That was a good trick, wasn't it?"

"No," said Little Mouse, who was cross that her brother's trick had worked so well.

"Come and have some tea," said Mrs Mouse. "I had to do something with all the pumpkin that Timmy scraped out so I've made a special treat. It's pumpkin pie!"

"Yippee!" said Little Mouse, smiling, and Timmy's pumpkin lantern smiled back.

Uncle Monty Mouse

Mrs Mouse had told Little Mouse that Uncle Monty was coming to stay.

"Now, I shall be far too busy to look after him all the time so you'll have to help me out," she said.

Uncle Monty arrived at eleven o'clock. He looked very stern.

"Oh dear, this isn't going to be much fun at all," said Little Mouse to herself. However, she tried to make Uncle Monty welcome and gave him a big cup of tea.

Little Mouse showed Uncle Monty the village green, the school,

Hollyholt Stores and the homes of all her friends. He didn't say much and Little Mouse found it hard work because nothing seemed to make her uncle happy.

Just then they saw Nippy Shrew, Little Bunny and Little Owl.

"Hello," called Little Mouse. "This is my Uncle Monty who is staying for two days." The friends gazed up at the strict-looking uncle. But Uncle Monty suddenly smiled and asked Little Mouse if she would run home to fetch his brown, shiny case. "I have something to show you," he told them, mysteriously.

Little Mouse was so surprised to see Uncle Monty smiling that she ran as fast as she could in case he was ill and it was medicine he needed from the case!

But when Uncle Monty opened his case, Little Mouse was amazed to see a big top hat, white gloves, a silver wand and lots of strange boxes and packages.

Uncle Monty put on the gloves and hat, tapped his wand and began to do all sorts of magic tricks. Little Owl flew off to let everyone know and soon a big crowd had gathered to watch Uncle Monty's special Magic Show.

Little Mouse was very proud of her Uncle.

"Thank you, Uncle Monty," she whispered as she helped him pack away at the end of the afternoon.

"Thank *you*, Little Mouse," said Uncle Monty. "Your friends were a great audience. I haven't enjoyed myself so much for years!"

And with a smile, he popped the big top hat on Little Mouse's head and let her wear it all the way home.

Uncle Monty's Farewell Surprise

It was the day that Uncle Monty was to set off for home after his short visit. Little Mouse was sad as she had really enjoyed all the magic tricks that he had performed.

"Uncle Monty, do you think you can teach me to do any of your magic tricks?" she asked.

"I'm afraid not," said her uncle, looking serious. "You see, I'm a member of the Magic Circle and we must never tell our secrets to anyone. After all, if we did everyone would know how the tricks worked and they wouldn't be so exciting, would they?"

Little Mouse agreed. "No, I suppose not. But couldn't you show me just one trick?"

Uncle Monty smiled. "Wait and see. Perhaps I do have one which you can learn."

Later that day Uncle Monty entertained the whole family. He pulled strings of handkerchiefs from empty boxes, made eggs appear from nowhere and blew up balloons into funny shapes.

Everyone was delighted and they clapped like mad. Little Mouse was so excited she forgot all about her uncle's promise.

It was only as he was about to leave that Little Mouse remembered. "Wait, Uncle!" she cried. "Don't forget to show me how to do a trick."

Uncle Monty stopped and put down his case. He took a piece of paper from his pocket and made it into a roll.

"Now hold this," he said, "and look through it at the wall. But keep both eyes open."

Little Mouse did as she was told.

"All right, now bring your paw up beside the tube."

"Oh!" squealed Little Mouse. "It looks like there's a hole in my

paw—and I can see right through it!"

"There you are," said Uncle Monty. "It's a trick you can practise on your friends."

As Little Mouse climbed into the bed that night, she told her mummy what a wonderful day she'd had.

"I'm glad," said Mrs Mouse. "Now just before you close your eyes, look under your pillow because I think Uncle Monty left something there for you."

Little Mouse looked and, tucked under her pillow was a special present—a tiny, silver, magic wand.

"Thank you, Uncle Monty," whispered Little Mouse, as she drifted off to sleep.

Auntie Flo's Bowl

One Christmas Auntie Flo gave Mr and Mrs Mouse a big bowl. It was a shiny blue and yellow colour and was shaped like a cockle shell.

"Thank you," said Mrs Mouse. "We'll put it here on the windowsill, shall we?" and she popped a few apples in it.

After Christmas, when Auntie had gone home, the Mouse family all agreed that it was the most horrible bowl they had ever seen, so they put it up in the attic. There it stayed—except when Auntie Flo came to visit. Then Mrs Mouse would polish it and put it back on the windowsill.

One day Timmy was hunting about in the attic for things to use in the school play.

"We've got an old trunk that you could use as a treasure chest," Mrs Mouse told him, when he said they were doing a play

about pirates hunting for treasure. "You'll probably find some other useful things too."

Timmy shone his torch round the attic and it lighted on something shiny. It was Auntie Flo's bowl.

"That would be perfect for pirate treasure," thought Timmy.

On the day of the play, Timmy went to school after tea to get ready. Mrs Mouse was busy dusting round before Auntie Flo arrived. She always came over for the school play.

"Don't forget to put her bowl out," said Mr Mouse. Mrs Mouse rushed up to the attic to fetch it, but she couldn't find it anywhere.

Auntie Flo didn't say anything, but Mrs Mouse felt sure she had noticed that the bowl was missing. But she soon forgot all about it as they settled into their seats and waited for the play to begin.

It went very well and Mrs Mouse felt very proud of Timmy as a pirate. When the treasure chest was found, Timmy opened the lid and pulled out a handful of treasure which he held up high for everyone to see. As he did so Auntie Flo gave a little cry.

"My bowl!" she said in a whisper to Mrs Mouse. She chuckled and said, "I wondered why it was missing, but I might have guessed it would be the prize treasure in the school play!"

"Now that it's so famous, I really think you ought to have it back, you know," Mrs Mouse told her.

"Well if you wouldn't mind . . ." said Auntie Flo.

So the next day she set off home with the bowl safely tucked under her arm. For ever afterwards she kept it in her living room and whenever friends came to see her she would tell them proudly how her bowl had been used as treasure in a play!

Little Mouse's Scarf

As winter drew near, Mr Mouse turned up his collar whenever he went out and said, "Brrr. It's cold out there today."

"Poor Daddy," thought Little Mouse. "He hasn't got a nice warm scarf. That's why he feels so cold." And she decided to knit him a scarf for his birthday next month.

She asked her mummy if she had any wool she could spare.

"If you look in the knitting box you'll find all the bits and pieces that are left over from my knitting," said Mrs Mouse.

Little Mouse found lots of wool in lots of different colours.

"What a bright and cheerful scarf this will make," she thought, as she chose red and orange, green and blue, purple and yellow. She took the wool back to her bedroom and started to knit.

"Daddy's a lot bigger than me," she thought, when the scarf was long enough to wrap round her neck. "I'd better do a bit more for him." So she knitted another few rows—and then a few more, just in case.

"That must be long enough now," she said to herself, laying it out along the bed. It looked beautiful, and Little Mouse was very proud of it. She wrapped it up carefully and put it away until Mr Mouse's birthday.

"Now what can this be?" he asked as he felt the parcel. "It's very soft and squashy.... A scarf! How lovely!"

He wrapped it twice round his neck, but it still reached the ground, so he wrapped it round once more. Now his mouth had disappeared, so Little Mouse could hardly hear him mumble, "Thank you," through the layers of wool.

"Oh dear," she said, feeling disappointed. "It's too big!"

"I have got a very good idea!" said Mrs Mouse. "Give the scarf to me." She disappeared upstairs with it and when she came back she was carrying, not one scarf, but two!

"There!" she said, handing one to Mr Mouse and one to Little Mouse. "Your scarf was long enough to cut into two. They should be just the right size."

And they were. Little Mouse felt very pleased when she and her daddy went out together that winter, both wearing their bright rainbow scarves.

The Last Christmas Tree

It was Christmas Eve and Mrs Mouse was making a last batch of mince pies while Mr Mouse put up the decorations.

"They look lovely, Daddy," said Little Mouse who had just come in. "But where's the Christmas tree?"

"Oh no," cried Mr Mouse. "I've forgotten to get one!"

"Never mind," said Mrs Mouse. "There are usually still a few left in Hollyholt Stores on Christmas Eve. You could pop down now."

"I'll go," said Little Mouse. She was soon running down the road and arrived, panting, at Hollyholt Stores.

"Hello, Mrs Badger! Have you got any Christmas trees?"

"I'm sorry, my dear," said Mrs Badger. "I sold the last one ten minutes ago. It was a very big one, too."

Little Mouse looked very sad.

"Do you mean you haven't got a tree at all?" asked Mrs Badger. "Why, that will never do. I tell you what, I've got a lot of holly left. You can take as much of that as you like. It isn't quite the same, but it's the best I can do."

Little Mouse set off home with the holly, feeling rather sad. It didn't seem like Christmas without a tree. As she got near to the Bunnies' house she could hear a lot of noise and she stopped to see what was happening.

"It's no good," said Little Bunny. "We'll never get it through the door."

He and Benny were struggling with a huge Christmas tree that filled the doorway.

"Hello, Little Mouse," called Little Bunny, seeing her standing sadly by the gate. "What's wrong?"

Little Mouse explained about the Christmas tree and Little Bunny suddenly gave a big smile.

"We had to buy a tree that's far too big, because it was the only one left," he explained. "We'll have to cut the top off to get it through our front door. You could have that as a little tree!"

Everyone watched Mr Bunny cut off the top branches. He was very careful, and soon there were two Christmas trees!

"Thank you so much," called Little Mouse, as she hurried home with her special little tree. "It's just *mouse*-size!"